PINKY and REX
and the
Mean Old Witch

PINKY and REX
and the
Mean Old Witch
by James Howe
illustrated by Melissa Sweet

Ready-to-Read

Simon Spotlight

First Aladdin Paperbacks edition September 1999
First Simon Spotlight paperback edition September 2012

Simon Spotlight
An imprint of Simon & Schuster
Children's Publishing Division
1230 Avenue of the Americas
New York, NY 10020

10 9 8 7 6 5 4 3

The Library of Congress has cataloged the hardcover edition as follows:
Howe, James, 1946-
Pinky and Rex and the mean old witch / by James Howe ; illustrated by Melissa Sweet.
p.   cm.
Summary: Pinky, Rex, and Amanda plot revenge on the bad-tempered
old woman who lives across the street, until Pinky realizes
that she is lonely and needs new friends.
ISBN 978-0-689-31617-3 (hc.)
[1. Neighborliness—Fiction. 2. Old age—Fiction.]
I. Sweet, Melissa, ill. II. Title.
PZ7.H83727Pm   1991
[E]—dc20
89-78204
ISBN 978-0-689-82879-9 (pbk.)
0812 LAK

To my niece, Rachel
—J.H.
To Mickey Connolly
—M.S.

Contents

Chapter 1

Monkey-in-the-Middle

"Not fair!"

Pinky and Rex were playing monkey-in-the-middle with Pinky's little sister, Amanda. As usual, Amanda was the monkey.

"Not fair," Amanda cried again, as the ball sailed over her head. "You big kids throw too high!"

"That's the idea," said Pinky. He
tossed the ball. It landed about ten
feet away from Rex.

"Pinky!" Rex shouted,
scrambling to get the ball before
Amanda could reach it. "Can't you
aim any better than that?"

Pinky shrugged his shoulders. "I

can't help it if my aim isn't so good."

"I just don't want the ball to roll
into Mrs. Morgan's yard," said Rex.
"You know what *she's* like."

"Uck," said Amanda. She stuck
out her tongue and didn't even
notice the ball as it whizzed past her.
"She's a witch!"

"Ssh," Pinky said. "Not so loud."

Pinky concentrated very hard on his aim. Then he hurled the ball with all his might. High into the air it went, high over Amanda's head. Amanda looked up. Rex looked up, too, as the ball flew over *her* head as well. "Oh, no," she said, when she saw where it was going to land.

The ball came down on the other side of Rex's driveway, just inside Mrs. Morgan's yard. It rolled another few feet before coming to a stop.

Pinky looked at Rex. Rex looked at Pinky. Amanda looked back and forth between them. "Well?" she said at last.

"I'm not going over there," said Rex. "I live next door to her, remember? I get in enough trouble with her."

"Don't look at me," Pinky told his sister.

"Are you *afraid*?" Amanda asked.

"Not exactly," said Pinky. But he didn't move. Neither did Rex.

"Big kids, humph!" Amanda said. "You're a couple of 'fraidy-cats." She stomped across Rex's yard and marched directly to the ball. No sooner had she touched it than the front door of the house flew open. A woman with wild gray hair charged down the steps, swinging a broom.

"Off!" she screamed. "Stay off my yard!"

Amanda dropped the ball and ran. She didn't say anything until the woman was gone. Then, in a very quiet voice, she said, "Mean old witch."

Chapter 2
Trouble

"She can't do that to us," said Rex. "That's *our* ball."

"Let's sue her!" Amanda cried.

"We've got to do something," Rex said. "She's the meanest person I ever saw. You can't even step on the corner of her yard by mistake without her running out and waving that broom around."

"She's a witch," Amanda repeated, as if the broom were proof of it.

"I guess we'd better get another ball," Pinky said with a sigh.

"No!" said Rex. "That's *our* ball, and I'm going to get it."

Rex inched her way across her own lawn before daring to set foot on her neighbor's. She took a deep breath, a big step, and then...

"I warned you!" Mrs. Morgan shouted. Down the steps she swooped again, holding the broom out at arm's <u>length</u> and jabbing the air in front of Rex. "Now, shoo, shoo," she said, as if Rex were a pesky fly. "Stay away or else!"

Rex grabbed the ball and ran.
"You're not nice!" she yelled.

Mrs. Morgan glared at Rex.
"Your mother will hear about this,
young lady," she said. "And if I ever
catch you on my property again, I'll
call the police! You mark my words."

"Do you really think she'll call the police?" Pinky asked, after the door slammed shut.

Rex shook her head. "She just says things like that."

"Are you going to get in trouble with your mom?" asked Amanda.

"I don't think so. My mother knows what Mrs. Morgan is like."

The three kids sat down on the grass. They didn't feel like playing ball anymore. After a few moments of silence, Pinky said, "We should teach her a lesson."

"Yeah," said Rex, her eyes brightening. "Let's show her she's not the *only* one who can be mean."

Chapter 3

Getting Even

Pinky, Rex, and Amanda tried to think of tricks they could play on the Mean Old Witch.

"I know!" said Rex. "Let's call her on the telephone and tell her she's won a million dollars. She'll get all excited, and then we'll call back and say it was all a mistake. Ha, ha!"

Amanda clapped her hands.
"That's funny, Rex!" she said.
"No, it isn't," said Pinky.
"Besides, she'd know she was talking
to a kid. She'd never believe it. What
if we leave a note under her door
that says 'You stink!'"
Amanda giggled.

"She deserves something meaner than that," said Rex.

"Well, what if we make signs and

put them all over the neighborhood?" Pinky suggested.

"What kind of signs?" asked Rex.

Pinky got excited just thinking about it. "Signs that say things like 'Mrs. Morgan Hates Kids!' Or, 'Watch Out for the Mean Old Witch of <u>Elm</u> Street!'"

Amanda jumped up. "Or, 'Wanted: Dead or Alive!'" she shouted.

"I don't think so," said Rex.

Pinky said, "Amanda, that's going a little *too* far."

Amanda crossed her arms. "You guys aren't any fun," she said. "I want to do signs."

"You don't even know how to write," Pinky pointed out.

Just then, Rex noticed Frank the mailman coming along the street in their direction. "I've got it!" she cried. "We'll spray Goopey-Goo in Mrs. Morgan's mailbox!"

Chapter 4

The Goopey-Goo Caper

The mailman delivered all the mail on the street and turned the corner at the end of the block. No one else was in sight. Pinky took his brand-new can of Goopey-Goo and crept toward Mrs. Morgan's front steps. He moved very slowly and very quietly. He had to be sure she didn't hear him or see him.

Rex and Amanda watched from where they were hiding in the bushes in front of Rex's house. Amanda had a hard time keeping herself from giggling.

"That's it," Rex said in a loud whisper. "You're almost there, Pinky."

Pinky looked up. Mrs. Morgan's mailbox was to the left of her front

door. He had one–two–three–four–
five steps to go up before he'd even
be close. What if they creaked? What
if someone saw him? He began to
wish it were nighttime instead of a
beautiful, sunshiny day. Any minute,
someone might come along and
shout, "Hey, Pinky, what are you
doing?"

As he moved up the steps, he gripped the can of Goopey-Goo tightly. One–two–three–four–five. He was up on Mrs. Morgan's porch. He hardly dared breathe. Slowly, he crept on all fours like a cat sneaking up on a bug.

He made it! He was right under Mrs. Morgan's mailbox. All he had to do was stand up, lift the top of the box, and...Pinky smiled to himself to think what a mess the Goopey-Goo would make of Mrs. Morgan's mail.

Just then, he heard something from inside the house! Pinky ducked down, then realized it was only the television set.

He peeked through Mrs. Morgan's window. The old woman

was sitting on a sofa, her hands folded on her lap. She wasn't even looking at the TV. She was just staring off into space. That's strange, Pinky thought. He wasn't sure why, but all of a sudden he felt sorry for her.

"Do it!" Rex hissed from the bush next door.

"What are you waiting for?"
Amanda whispered.

Pinky started to stand up. He was
ready to spray the Goopey-Goo into
Mrs. Morgan's mailbox. Then he
glanced through her window again.
Why was she sitting all alone in a dark
house on such a beautiful day?

25

As quietly as he could, he crept back down the steps.

"She saw me, she saw me!" he cried when he was back in Rex's yard. "We'll have to try it again tomorrow!"

Rex looked over at Mrs. Morgan's house. "If she saw you," she asked, "why isn't she out here waving her broom?"

Pinky didn't have an answer.

Chapter 5

Pinky and His Father

That evening after dinner, Pinky was baking cookies with his father.

"You know the old woman who lives across the street?" Pinky asked.

"Mrs. Morgan?" said his father.

Pinky nodded. "We call her the Mean Old Witch."

"That isn't very nice."

27

"I know," Pinky said. "But she really *is* mean. Today, she chased us off her yard, and all we wanted to do was get our ball. We didn't *want* it to roll over there. It just happened. She even swung a broom at us!"

"Well," said Pinky's father, opening the oven door to take out one batch of cookies and put in another, "it wasn't right of her to swing a broom at you. But people make her nervous, I think. Especially kids. Maybe the best thing to do is stay away from her."

Pinky sat down at the kitchen table. "Why is she like that?" he asked. "Was she born mean?"

His father laughed. "Nobody's born mean," he said. "Life just makes people that way sometimes. Mrs. Morgan's husband died a long time ago. They never had any children. I guess she doesn't have anyone left to love, Pinky. Maybe she's forgotten how."

Chapter 6
Pinky's New Plan

The next day, Pinky told Rex and Amanda that he had a new plan to get even with Mrs. Morgan.

"What is it?" Rex asked. "What's your plan?"

"You'll see," said Pinky. "It's a surprise."

Rex noticed that Pinky was
carrying a small brown bag. "What do
you have in there?" she asked.

Pinky said again, "You'll see."

"Please, Pinky," Amanda whined,
"tell us what's in the bag."

"Is it worms?" said Rex, wrinkling up her nose in glee.

"Is it garbage?" Amanda asked. She started to giggle.

Pinky just said, "Follow me."

He started walking toward Mrs. Morgan's house.

"Pinky!" said Rex. "If she sees us coming, she'll be out here with her broom. We'd better sneak up on her."

But Pinky kept walking. He walked straight up the Mean Old Witch's front walk and right up the steps of her house. Rex and Amanda stopped in the middle of the sidewalk. They couldn't believe what Pinky was doing.

"Oh, are we going to get in trouble," Rex groaned.

Pinky rang the bell.

When the old woman appeared
at the door, she stared in disbelief.
"What do *you* want?" she snapped at
Pinky. She looked out at the two girls
standing on the sidewalk. "I warned
you kids," she said. "I told you I
would call the police the next time

you set foot on my property. Well,
now I'm going to do it!"

She started to close the door.
Pinky swallowed hard and said, "We
brought you some cookies."

Rex and Amanda were almost as
shocked as Mrs. Morgan.

"Cookies?" the old woman said, turning. "What do I want with cookies? Is this a trick?"

"No, ma'am," said Pinky. "My father and I made some chocolate-chip cookies last night. And I thought you might like some."

Mrs. Morgan stood stock-still in her dark, dark house for what seemed like a long time. Then she opened the door a crack and reached out her hand. "Let me see that," she said.

Pinky gave her the bag and watched her open it and look inside. "You made these with your father?" she asked.

"Yes, ma'am."

"And you want me to have them?"

"Yes, ma'am."

The woman glanced at Pinky,
then back at the bag in her hands.
"My, my," he heard her say, as she
closed the door and went back inside
the house. "It's been a long time
since I had any homemade cookies."

"She could have said thank you," said Amanda, when the three kids were safely back in Rex's yard.

"Any *decent* grown-up would have offered to share," Rex added.

"See?" Amanda said. "She's still a witch."

But later that afternoon, when their ball rolled into the yard next door and Pinky went to get it, Mrs. Morgan did not come running out swinging a broom.

"Maybe next time she'll say thank you," said Pinky, returning with the ball. "Maybe next time she'll even invite us in."

"*Next* time?" Rex said.

"Sure," said Pinky. "I only gave her six cookies. They can't last forever."

Pinky and Rex looked over at Mrs. Morgan's house. They saw that she was watching them from her window. After a moment, they went back to their game of monkey-in-the-middle.

As usual, Amanda was the monkey.